THE TERROR IN THE AIR

BY

ARTHUR B. REEVE

British Library Cataloguing-in-Publication Data
A catalogue record for this book is available from the
British Library

Arthur Benjamin Reeve

Arthur Benjamin Reeve was born on 15th October 1880 in New York, USA.

Reeve received his University education at Princeton and upon graduating enrolled at the New York Law School. However, his career was not destined to be in the field of Law. Between 1910 and 1918 he produced 82 short stories for Cosmopolitan magazine featuring his super-sleuth Professor Craig Kennedy. Kennedy is sometimes referred to as "The American Sherlock Holmes" due to his astounding ability at crime solving and his Watson-like sidekick Walter Jameson, a newspaper reporter. These characters featured in 18 novels, some of which were pseudo-novels stitched together from various short stories.

During this period he also began authoring screenplays, beginning with *The Exploits of Elaine* (1914). By the end of this decade his film career was at its peak with his name appearing on seven films, most of them serials and three of them starring Harry Houdini. Due to the film industry's migration to the west coast of America and Reeve's desire to remain in the east he produced less and less work for film. However, in 1927 he entered into a contract to write film scenarios for notorious millionaire-murderer, Harry K. Thaw, on the subject of fake spiritualists. The deal resulted in a lawsuit when Thaw refused to pay. In late 1928, Reeve declared bankruptcy.

Reeve continued to write detective stories for pulp magazines, but also covered many celebrated crime cases for various newspapers, including the murder of William Desmond Taylor, and the trial of Lindbergh baby kidnapper, Bruno Hauptmann. During the 1930s he became an anti-rackets crusader and produced a work of history on the subject titled *The Golden Age of Crime* (1931).

In 1932 he moved to Trenton to be near his alma mater. He died on 9th August 1936.

THE TERROR IN THE AIR

"There's something queer about these aeroplane accidents at Belmore Park," mused Kennedy, one evening, as his eye caught a big headline in the last edition of the Star, which I had brought uptown with me.

"Queer?" I echoed. "Unfortunate, terrible, but hardly queer. Why, it is a common saying among the aeronauts that if they keep at it long enough they will all lose their lives."

"Yes, I know that," rejoined Kennedy; "but, Walter, have you noticed that all these accidents have happened to Norton's new gyroscope machines?"

"Well, what of that" I replied. "Isn't it just barely possible that Norton is on the wrong track in applying the gyroscope to an aeroplane? I can't say I know much about either the gyroscope or the aeroplane, but from what I hear the fellows at the office say it would seem to me that the gyroscope is a pretty good thing to keep off an aeroplane, not to put on it."

"Why?" asked Kennedy blandly.

"Well, it seems to me, from what the experts say, that anything which tends to keep your machine in one position is just what you don't want in an aeroplane. What surprises them, they say, is that the thing seems to work so well up to a certain point--that the accidents don't happen sooner. Why, our man on the aviation field tells me that when that poor fellow Browne was killed he had all but succeeded in bringing his machine to a dead stop in the air. In other words, he would have won the Brooks Prize for perfect motionlessness in one place. And then Herrick, the day before, was going about seventy miles an hour when he collapsed. They said it was heart failure. But to-night another expert says in the Star--here, I'll read it: 'The real cause was carbonic-acid-gas poisoning due to the pressure on the mouth from driving fast through the air, and the consequent inability to expel the poisoned air which had been breathed. Air once breathed is practically carbonic-acid-gas. When one is passing rapidly through the air this carbonic-acid-gas is pushed back into the lungs, and only a little can get away because of the rush of air pressure into the mouth. So it is rebreathed, and the result is gradual carbonic-acid-gas poisoning, which produces a kind of narcotic sleep.'"

"Then it wasn't the gyroscope in that case?" said Kennedy with a rising inflection.

"No," I admitted reluctantly, "perhaps not."

I could see that I had been rash in talking so long. Kennedy had only been sounding me to see what the newspapers thought of it. His next remark was characteristic.

"Norton has asked me to look into the thing," he said quietly. "If his invention is a failure, he is a ruined man. All his money is in it, he is suing a man for infringing on his

4

patent, and he is liable for damages to the heirs, according to his agreement with Browne and Herrick. I have known Norton some time; in fact, he worked out his ideas at the university physical laboratory. I have flown in his machine, and it is the most marvellous biplane I ever saw. Walter, I want you to get a Belmore Park assignment from the Star and go out to the aviation meet with me to-morrow. I'll take you on the field, around the machines--you can get enough local colour to do a dozen Star specials later on. I may add that devising a flying-machine capable of remaining stationary in the air means a revolution that will relegate all other machines to the scrap-heap. From a military point of view it is the one thing necessary to make the aeroplane the superior in every respect to the dirigible."

The regular contests did not begin until the afternoon, but Kennedy and I decided to make a day of it, and early the next morning we were speeding out to the park where the flights were being held.

We found Charles Norton, the inventor, anxiously at work with his mechanicians in the big temporary shed that had been accorded him, and was dignified with the name of hangar.

"I knew you would come, Professor," he exclaimed, running forward to meet us.

"Of course," echoed Kennedy. "I'm too much interested in this invention of yours not to help you, Norton. You know what I've always thought of it--I've told you often that it is the most important advance since the original discovery by the Wrights that the aeroplane could be balanced by warping the planes."

"I'm just fixing up my third machine," said Norton. "If anything happens to it, I shall lose the prize, at least as far as this meet is concerned, for I don't believe I shall get my fourth and newest model from the makers in time. Anyhow, if I did I couldn't pay for it--I am ruined, if I don't win that twenty-five-thousand-dollar Brooks Prize. And, besides, a couple of army men are coming to inspect my aeroplane and report to the War Department on it. I'd have stood a good chance of selling it, I think, if my flights here had been like the trials you saw. But, Kennedy," he added, and his face was drawn and tragic, "I'd drop the whole thing if I didn't know I was right. Two men dead--think of it. Why, even the newspapers are beginning to call me a cold, heartless, scientific crank, to keep on. But I'll show them--this afternoon I'm going to fly myself. I'm not afraid to go anywhere I send my men. I'll die before I'll admit I'm beaten."

It was easy to see why Kennedy was fascinated by a man of Norton's type. Anyone would have been. It was not foolhardiness. It was dogged determination, faith in himself and in his own ability to triumph over every obstacle.

We now slowly entered the shed where two men were working over Norton's biplane. One of the men was a

Frenchman, Jaurette, who had worked with Farman, a silent, dark-browed, weatherbeaten fellow with a sort of sullen politeness. The other man was an American, Roy Sinclair, a tall, lithe, wiry chap with a seamed and furrowed face and a loose-jointed but very deft manner which marked him a born bird-man. Norton's third aviator, Humphreys, who was not to fly that day, much to his relief, was reading a paper in the back of the shed.

We were introduced to him, and be seemed to be a very companionable sort of fellow, though not given to talking.

"Mr. Norton," he said, after the introduction, "there's quite an account of your injunction against Delanne in this paper. It doesn't seem to be very friendly," he added, indicating the article.

Norton read it and frowned. "Humph! I'll show them yet that my application of the gyroscope is patentable. Delanne will put me into 'interference' in the patent office, as the lawyers call it, will he? Well, I filed a 'caveat' over a year and a half ago. If I'm wrong, he's wrong, and all gyroscope patents are wrong, and if I'm right, by George, I'm first in the field. That's so, isn't it?" he appealed to Kennedy.

Kennedy shrugged his shoulders non-committally, as if he had never heard of the patent office or the gyroscope in his life. The men were listening, whether or not from loyalty I could not tell.

"Let us see your gyroplane, I mean aeroscope--whatever it is you call it," asked Kennedy.

Norton took the cue. "Now you newspaper men are the first that I've allowed in here," he said. "Can I trust your word of honour not to publish a line except such as I O.K. after you write it?"

We promised.

As Norton directed, the mechanicians wheeled the aeroplane out on the field in front of the shed. No one was about.

"Now this is the gyroscope," began Norton, pointing out a thing encased in an aluminum sheath, which weighed, all told, perhaps fourteen or fifteen pounds. "You see, the gyroscope is really a flywheel mounted on gimbals and can turn on any of its angles so that it can assume any angle in space. When it's at rest like this you can turn it easily. But when set revolving it tends to persist always in the plane in which it was started rotating."

I took hold of it, and it did turn readily in any direction. I could feel the heavy little flywheel inside.

"There is a pretty high vacuum in that aluminum case," went on Norton. "There's very little friction on that account. The power to rotate the flywheel is obtained from this little dynamo here, run by the gas-engine which also turns the propellers of the aeroplane."

"But suppose the engine stops, how about the gyroscope?" I asked sceptically.

"It will go right on for several minutes. You know, the Brennan monorail car will stand up some time after the power is shut off. And I carry a small storage-battery that will run it for some time, too. That's all been guarded against."

Jaurette cranked the engine, a seven-cylindered affair, with the cylinders sticking out like the spokes of a wheel without a rim. The propellers turned so fast that I could not see the blades--turned with that strong, steady, fierce droning buzz that can be heard a long distance and which is a thrilling sound to hear. Norton reached over and attached the little dynamo, at the same time setting the gyroscope at its proper angle and starting it.

"This is the mechanical brain of my new flier," he remarked, patting the aluminum case lovingly. "You can look in through this little window in the case and see the flywheel inside revolving--ten thousand revolutions a minute. Press down on the gyroscope," he shouted to me.

As I placed both hands on the case of the apparently frail little instrument, he added, "You remember how easily you moved it just a moment ago."

I pressed down with all my might. Then I literally raised myself off my feet, and my whole weight was on the gyroscope. That uncanny little instrument seemed to resent--yes, that's the word, resent--my touch. It was almost human in the resentment, too. Far from yielding to me, it actually rose on the side I was pressing down!

The men who were watching me laughed at the puzzled look on my face.

I took my hands off, and the gyroscope leisurely and nonchalantly went back to its original position.

"That's the property we use, applied to the rudder and the ailerons--those flat planes between the large main planes. That gives automatic stability to the machine," continued Norton. "I'm not going to explain how it is done--it is in the combination of the various parts that I have discovered the basic principle, and I'm not going to talk about it till the thing is settled by the courts. But it is there, and the court will see it, and I'll prove that Delanne is a fraud--a fraud when he says that my combination isn't patentable and isn't practicable even at that. The truth is that his device as it stands isn't practicable, and, besides, if he makes it so it infringes on mine. Would you like to take a flight with me?"

I looked at Kennedy, and a vision of the wreckage of the two previous accidents, as the Star photographer had snapped them, flashed across my mind. But Kennedy was too quick for me.

"Yes," he answered. "A short flight. No stunts."

We took our seats by Norton, I, at least, with some misgiving. Gently the machine rose into the air. The sensation was delightful. The fresh air of the morning came with a stinging rush to my face. Below I could see the earth sweeping past as if it were a moving-picture film. Above the continuous roar of the engine and propeller Norton indicated to Kennedy the automatic balancing of the gyroscope as it bent the ailerons.

"Could you fly in this machine without the gyroscope at all?" yelled Kennedy. The noise was deafening, conversation almost impossible. Though sitting side by side he had to repeat his remark twice to Norton.

"Yes," called back Norton. Reaching back of him, he pointed out the way to detach the gyroscope and put a sort of brake on it that stopped its revolutions almost instantly. "It's a ticklish job to change in the air," he shouted. "It can be done, but it's safer to land and do it."

The flight was soon over, and we stood admiring the machine while Norton expatiated on the compactness of his little dynamo.

"What have you done with the wrecks of the other machines?" inquired Kennedy at length.

"They are stored in a shed down near the railroad station. They are just a mass of junk, though there are some parts that I can use, so I'll ship them back to the factory."

"Might I have a look at them?"

"Surely. I'll give you the key. Sorry I can't go myself, but I want to be sure everything is all right for my flight this afternoon."

It was a long walk over to the shed near the station, and, together with our examination of the wrecked machines, it took us the rest of the morning. Craig carefully turned over the wreckage. It seemed a hopeless quest to me, but I fancied that to him it merely presented new problems for his deductive and scientific mind.

"These gyroscopes are out of business for good," he remarked as he glanced at the dented and battered aluminum cases. "But there doesn't seem to be anything wrong with them except what would naturally happen in such accidents."

For my part I felt a sort of awe at the mass of wreckage in which Browne and Herrick had been killed. It was to me more than a tangled mass of wires and splinters. Two human lives had been snuffed out in it.

"The engines are a mass of scrap; see how the cylinders are bent and twisted," remarked Kennedy with great interest. "The gasoline-tank is intact, but dented out of shape. No explosion there. And look at this dynamo. Why, the wires in it are actually fused together. The insulation has been completely burned off. I wonder what could have caused that?"

Kennedy continued to regard the tangled mass thoughtfully for some time, then locked the door, and we strolled back to the grand stand on our side of the field. Already the crowd had begun to collect. Across the field we could see the various machines in front of their hangars with the men working on them. The buzz of the engines was wafted across by the light summer breeze as if a thousand cicadas had broken loose to predict warm weather.

Two machines were already in flight, a little yellow Demoiselle, scurrying around close to the earth like a frightened hen, and a Bleriot, high overhead, making slow and graceful turns like a huge bird.

Kennedy and I stopped before the little wireless telegraph station of the signal corps in front of the grand stand and watched the operator working over his instruments.

"There it is again," muttered the operator angrily.

"What's the matter?" asked Kennedy. "Amateurs interfering with you?"

The man nodded a reply, shaking his head with the telephone-like receiver, viciously. He continued to adjust his apparatus.

"Confound it!" he exclaimed. "Yes, that fellow has been jamming me for the past two days off and on, every time I get ready to send or receive a message. Williams is going up with a Wright machine equipped with wireless apparatus in a minute, and this fellow won't get out of the way. By Jove, though, those are powerful impulses of his.

Hear that crackling? I've never been interfered with so in my experience. Touch that screen door with your knife."

Kennedy did so, and elicited large sparks with quite a tingle of a shock.

"Yesterday and the day before it was so bad we had to give up attempting to communicate with Williams," continued the operator. "It was worse than trying to work in a thunder-shower. That's the time we get our troubles, when the air is overcharged with electricity, as it is now."

"That's interesting," remarked Kennedy.

"Interesting?" flashed back the operator, angrily noting the condition in his "log book."

"Maybe it is, but I call it darned mean. It's almost like trying to work in a power station."

"Indeed?" queried Kennedy. "I beg your pardon--I was only looking at it from the purely scientific point of view. Who is it, do you suppose?"

"How do I know? Some amateur, I guess. No professional would butt in this way."

Kennedy took a leaf out of his note-book and wrote a short message which he gave to a boy to deliver to Norton.

"Detach your gyroscope and dynamo," it read. "Leave them in the hangar. Fly without them this afternoon, and see what happens. No use to try for the prize to-day. Kennedy."

We sauntered out on the open part of the field, back of the fence and to the side of the stands, and watched the fliers for a few moments. Three were in the air now, and I could see Norton and his men getting ready.

The boy with the message was going rapidly across the field. Kennedy was impatiently watching him. It was too far off to see just what they were doing, but as Norton seemed to get down out of his seat in the aeroplane when the boy arrived, and it was wheeled back into the shed, I gathered that he was detaching the gyroscope and was going to make the flight without it, as Kennedy had requested.

In a few minutes it was again wheeled out.

The crowd, which had been waiting especially to see Norton, applauded.

"Come, Walter," exclaimed Kennedy, "let's go up there on the roof of the stand where we can see better. There's a platform and railing, I see."

His pass allowed him to go anywhere on the field, so in a few moments we were up on the roof.

It was a fascinating vantage-point, and I was so deeply engrossed between watching the crowd below, the bird-men in the air, and the machines waiting across the field that I totally neglected to notice what Kennedy was doing. When I did, I saw that he had deliberately turned his back on the aviation field, and was anxiously, scanning the country back of us.

"What are you looking for?" I asked. "Turn around. I think Norton is just about to fly."

"Watch him then," answered Craig. "Tell me when he gets in the air."

Just then Norton's aeroplane rose gently from the field. A wild shout of applause came from the people below us, at the heroism of the man who dared to fly this new and apparently fated machine. It was succeeded by a breathless, deathly calm, as if after the first burst of enthusiasm the crowd had suddenly realised the danger of the intrepid aviator. Would Norton add a third to the fatalities of the meet?

Suddenly Kennedy jerked my arm. "Walter, look over there across the road back of us--at the old weatherbeaten barn. I mean the one next to that yellow house. What do you see?"

"Nothing, except that on the peak of the roof there is a pole that looks like the short stub of a small wireless mast. I should say there was a boy connected with that barn, a boy who has read a book on wireless for beginners."

"Maybe," said Kennedy. "But is that all you see? Look up in the little window of the gable, the one with the closed shutter."

I looked carefully. "It seems to me that I saw a gleam of something bright at the top of the shutter, Craig," I ventured. "A spark or a flash."

"It must be a bright spark, for the sun is shining brightly," mused Craig.

"Oh, maybe it's the small boy with a looking-glass. I can remember when I used to get behind such a window and shine a glass into the darkened room of my neighbours across the street."

I had really said that half in raillery, for I was at a loss to account in any other way for the light, but I was surprised to see how eagerly Craig accepted it.

"Perhaps you are right, in a way," he assented. "I guess it isn't a spark, after all. Yes, it must be the reflection of the sun on a piece of glass--the angles are just about right for it. Anyhow it caught my eye. Still, I believe that barn will bear watching."

Whatever his suspicions, Craig kept them to himself, and descended. At the same time Norton gently dropped back to earth in front of his hangar, not ten feet from the spot where he started. The applause was deafening, as the machine was again wheeled into the shed safely.

Kennedy and I pushed through the crowd to the wireless operator.

"How's she working?" inquired Craig.

"Rotten," replied the operator sullenly. "It was worse than ever about five minutes ago. It's much better now, almost normal again."

Just then the messenger-boy, who had been hunting through the crowd for us, handed Kennedy a note. It was merely a scrawl from Norton:

"Everything seems fine. Am going to try her next with the gyroscope. NORTON."

"Boy," exclaimed Craig, "has Cdr. Norton a telephone?"

"No, sir, only that hangar at the end has a telephone."

"Well, you run across that field as fast as your legs can carry you and tell him if he values his life not to do it."

"Not to do what, sir?"

"Don't stand there, youngster. Run! Tell him not to fly with that gyroscope. There's a five-spot in it if you get over there before he starts."

Even as he spoke the Norton aeroplane was wheeled out again. In a minute Norton had climbed up into his seat and was testing the levers.

Would the boy reach him in time? He was half across the field, waving his arms like mad. But apparently Norton and his men were too engrossed in their machine to pay attention.

"Good heavens!" exclaimed Craig. "He's going to try it. Run, boy, run!" he cried, although the boy was now far out of hearing.

Across the field we could hear now the quick staccato chug-chug of the engine. Slowly Norton's aeroplane, this time really equipped with the gyroscope, rose from the field and circled over toward us. Craig frantically signalled to him to come down, but of course Norton could not have seen him in the crowd. As for the crowd, they looked askance at Kennedy, as if he had taken leave of his senses.

I heard the wireless operator cursing the way his receiver was acting.

Higher and higher Norton went in one spiral after another, those spirals which his gyroscope had already made famous.

The man with the megaphone in front of the judge's stand announced in hollow tones that Mr. Norton had given notice that he would try for the Brooks Prize for stationary equilibrium.

Kennedy and I stood speechless, helpless, appalled.

Slower and slower went the aeroplane. It seemed to hover just like the big mechanical bird that it was.

Kennedy was anxiously watching the judges with one eye and Norton with the other. A few in the crowd could no longer restrain their applause. I remember that the wireless back of us was spluttering and crackling like mad.

All of a sudden a groan swept over the crowd. Something was wrong with Norton. His aeroplane was swooping downward at a terrific rate. Would he be able to control it? I held my breath and gripped Kennedy by the arm. Down, down came Norton, frantically fighting by main strength, it seemed to me, to warp the planes so that their surface might catch the air and check his descent.

"He's trying to detach the gyroscope," whispered Craig hoarsely.

The football helmet which Norton wore blew off and fell more rapidly than the plane. I shut my eyes. But Kennedy's next exclamation caused me quickly to open them again.

"He'll make it, after all!"

Somehow Norton had regained partial control of his machine, but it was still swooping down at a tremendous pace toward the level centre of the field.

There was a crash as it struck the ground in a cloud of dust.

With a leap Kennedy had cleared the fence and was running toward Norton. Two men from the judge's stand were ahead of us, but except for them we were the first to reach him. The men were tearing frantically at the tangled framework, trying to lift it off Norton, who lay pale and motionless, pinned under it. The machine was not so badly damaged, after all, but that together we could lift it bodily off him.

A doctor ran out from the crowd and hastily put his ear to Norton's chest. No one spoke, but we all scanned the doctor's face anxiously.

"Just stunned--he'll be all right in a moment. Get some water," he said.

Kennedy pulled my arm. "Look at the gyroscope dynamo," he whispered.

I looked. Like the other two which we had seen, it also was a wreck. The insulation was burned off the wires, the wires were fused together, and the storage-battery looked as if it had been burned out.

A flicker of the eyelid and Norton seemed to regain some degree of consciousness. He was living over again the ages that had passed during the seconds of his terrible fall.

"Will they never stop? Oh, those sparks, those sparks! I can't disconnect it. Sparks, more sparks--will they never--" So he rambled on. It was fearsome to hear him.

But Kennedy was now sure that Norton was safe and in good hands, and he hurried back in the direction of the grand stand. I followed. Flying was over for that day, and the people were filing slowly out toward the railroad station where the special trains were waiting. We stopped at the wireless station for a moment.

"Is it true that Norton will recover?" inquired the operator.

"Yes. He was only stunned, thank Heaven! Did you keep a record of the antics of your receiver since I saw you last?"

"Yes, sir. And I made a copy for you. By the way, it's working all right now when I don't want it. If Williams was only in the air now I'd give you a good demonstration of communicating with an aeroplane," continued the operator as he prepared to leave.

Kennedy thanked him for the record and carefully folded it. Joining the crowd, we pushed our way out, but instead of going down to the station with them, Kennedy turned toward the barn and the yellow house.

For some time we waited about casually, but nothing occurred. At length Kennedy walked up to the shed. The door was closed and double padlocked. He knocked, but there was no answer.

Just then a man appeared on the porch of the yellow house. Seeing us, he beckoned. As we approached he shouted, "He's gone for the day!"

"Has he a city address--any place I could reach him to-night?" asked Craig.

"I don't know. He hired the barn from me for two weeks and paid in advance. He told me if I wanted to address him the best way was 'Dr. K. Lamar, General Delivery, New York City.'"

"Ah, then I suppose I had better write to him," said Kennedy, apparently much gratified to learn the name. "I presume he'll be taking away his apparatus soon?"

"Can't say. There's enough of it. Cy Smith--he's in the electric light company up to the village--says the doctor has used a powerful lot of current. He's good pay, though he's awful closemouthed. Flying's over for to-day, ain't it? Was that feller much hurt?"

"No, he'll be all right to-morrow. I think he'll fly again. The machine's in pretty good condition. He's bound to win that prize. Good-bye."

As he walked away I remarked, "How do you know Norton will fly again?"

"I don't," answered Kennedy, "but I think that either he or Humphreys will. I wanted to see that this Lamar believes it anyhow. By the way, Walter, do you think you could grab a wire here and 'phone in a story to the Star that Norton isn't much hurt and will probably be able to fly to-morrow? Try to get the City News Association, too, so that all the papers will have it. I don't care about risking the general delivery--perhaps Lamar won't call for any mail, but he certainly will read the papers. Put it in the form of an interview with Norton--I'll see that it is all right and that there is no come-back. Norton will stand for it when I tell him my scheme."

I caught the Star just in time for the last edition, and some of the other papers that had later editions also had the story. Of course all the morning papers had it.

Norton spent the night in the Mineola Hospital. He didn't really need to stay, but the doctor said it would be best in case some internal injury had been overlooked. Meanwhile Kennedy took charge of the hangar where the injured machine was. The men had been in a sort of panic; Humphrey could not be found, and the only reason, I think, why the two mechanicians stayed was because something was due them on their pay.

Kennedy wrote them out personal checks for their respective amounts, but dated them two days ahead to insure their staying. He threw off all disguise now and with authority from Norton directed the repairing of the machine. Fortunately it was in pretty good condition. The broken part was the skids, not the essential parts of the machine. As for the gyroscope, there were plenty of them and another dynamo, and it was a very simple thing to replace the old one that had been destroyed.

Sinclair worked with a will, far past his regular hours. Jaurette also worked, though one could hardly say with a will. In fact, most of the work was done by Sinclair and Kennedy, with Jaurette sullenly grumbling, mostly in French under his breath. I did not like the fellow and was suspicious of him. I thought I noticed that Kennedy did not allow him to do much of the work, either, though that may have been for the reason that Kennedy never asked anyone to help him who seemed unwilling.

"There," exclaimed Craig about ten o'clock. "If we want to get back to the city in any kind of time to-night we had better quit. Sinclair, I think you can finish repairing these skids in the morning."

We locked up the hangar and hurried across to the station. It was late when we arrived in New York, but

Kennedy insisted on posting off up to his laboratory, leaving me to run down to the Star office to make sure that our story was all right for the morning papers.

I did not see him until morning, when a large touring-car drove up. Kennedy routed me out of bed. In the tonneau of the car was a huge package carefully wrapped up.

"Something I worked on for a couple of hours last night," explained Craig, patting it. "If this doesn't solve the problem then I'll give it up."

I was burning with curiosity, but somehow, by a perverse association of ideas, I merely reproached Kennedy for not taking enough rest.

"Oh," he smiled. "If I hadn't been working last night, Walter, I couldn't have rested at all for thinking about it."

When we arrived at the field Norton was already there with his head bandaged. I thought him a little pale, but otherwise all right. Jaurette was sulking, but Sinclair had finished the repairs and was busily engaged in going over every bolt and wire. Humphreys had sent word that he had another offer and had not shown up.

"We must find him," exclaimed Kennedy. "I want him to make a flight to-day. His contract calls for it."

"I can do it, Kennedy," asserted Norton. "See, I'm all right."

He picked up two pieces of wire and held them at arm's length, bringing them together, tip to tip, in front of him just to show us how he could control his nerves.

"And I'll be better yet by this afternoon," he added. "I can do that stunt with the points of pins then."

Kennedy shook his head gravely, but Norton insisted, and finally Kennedy agreed to give up wasting time trying to locate Humphreys. After that he and Norton had a long whispered conference in which Kennedy seemed to be unfolding a scheme.

"I understand," said Norton at length, "you want me to put this sheet-lead cover over the dynamo and battery first. Then you want me to take the cover off, and also to detach the gyroscope, and to fly without using it. Is that it?"

"Yes," assented Craig. "I will be on the roof of the grand stand. The signal will be three waves of my hat repeated till I see you get it."

After a quick luncheon we went up to our vantage-point. On the way Kennedy had spoken to the head of the Pinkertons engaged by the management for the meet, and had also dropped in to see the wireless operator to ask him to send up a messenger if he saw the same phenomena as he had observed the day before.

On the roof Kennedy took from his pocket a little instrument with a needle which trembled back and forth over a dial. It was nearing the time for the start of the day's flying, and the aeroplanes were getting ready. Kennedy was calmly biting a cigar, casting occasional glances at the needle as it oscillated. Suddenly, as Williams rose in the Wright machine, the needle swung quickly and pointed straight at the aviation field, vibrating through a small area, back and forth.

"The operator is getting his apparatus ready to signal to Williams," remarked Craig. "This is an apparatus called an ondometer. It tells you the direction and something of the magnitude of the Hertzian waves used in wireless."

Five or ten minutes passed. Norton was getting ready to fly. I could see through my field glass that he was putting something over his gyroscope and over the dynamo, but could not quite make out what it was. His machine seemed to leap up in the air as if eager to redeem itself. Norton with his white-bandaged head was the hero of the hour. No sooner had his aeroplane got up over the level of the trees than I heard a quick exclamation from Craig.

"Look at the needle, Walter!" he cried. "As soon as Norton got into the air it shot around directly opposite to the wireless station, and now it is pointing--"

We raised our eyes in the direction which it indicated. It was precisely in line with the weather-beaten barn.

I gasped. What did it mean? Did it mean in some way another accident to Norton--perhaps fatal this time? Why had Kennedy allowed him to try it to-day when there was even a suspicion that some nameless terror was abroad in the air? Quickly I turned to see if Norton was all right. Yes, there he was, circling above us in a series of wide spirals, climbing up, up. Now he seemed almost to stop, to hover motionless. He was motionless. His engine had been cut out, and I could see his propeller stopped. He was riding as a ship rides on the ocean.

A boy ran up the ladder to the roof. Kennedy unfolded the note and shoved it into my hands. It was from the operator.

"Wireless out of business again. Curse that fellow who is butting in. Am keeping record," was all it said.

I shot a glance of inquiry at Kennedy, but he was paying no attention now to anything but Norton. He held his watch in his hand.

"Walter," he ejaculated as he snapped it shut, "it has now been seven minutes and a half since he stopped his propeller. The Brooks Prize calls for five minutes only. Norton has exceeded it fifty per cent. Here goes."

With his hat in his hand he waved three times and stopped. Then he repeated the process.

At the third time the aeroplane seemed to give a start. The propeller began to revolve, Norton starting it on the compression successfully. Slowly he circled down again. Toward the end of the descent he stopped the engine and volplaned, or coasted, to the ground, landing gently in front of his hangar.

A wild cheer rose into the air from the crowd below us. All eyes were riveted on the activity about Norton's biplane. They were doing something to it. Whatever it was, it was finished in a minute and the men were standing again at a respectful distance from the propellers. Again Norton was in the air. As he rose above the field Kennedy gave a last glance at his ondometer and sprang down the ladder. I followed closely. Back of the crowd he hurried, down the walk to the entrance near the railroad station. The man in charge of the Pinkertons was at the gate with two other men, apparently waiting.

"Come on!" shouted Craig.

We four followed him as fast as we could. He turned in at the lane running up to the yellow house, so as to approach the barn from the rear, unobserved.

"Quietly, now," he cautioned.

We were now at the door of the barn. A curious crackling, snapping noise issued. Craig gently tried the door. It was bolted on the inside. As many of us as could threw ourselves like a human catapult against it. It yielded.

Inside I saw a sheet of flame fifteen or twenty feet long--it was a veritable artificial bolt of lightning. A man with a telescope had been peering out of the window, but now was facing us in surprise.

"Lamar," shouted Kennedy, drawing a pistol, "one motion of your hand and you are a dead man. Stand still where you are. You are caught red-handed."

The rest of us shrank back in momentary fear of the gigantic forces of nature which seemed let loose in the room. The thought, in my mind at least, was: Suppose this arch-fiend should turn his deadly power on us?

Kennedy saw us from the corner of his eye. "Don't be afraid," he said with just a curl to his lip. "I've seen all this before. It won't hurt you. It's a high frequency current. The man has simply appropriated the invention of Mr. Nikola Tesla. Seize him. He won't struggle. I've got him covered."

Two burly Pinkertons leaped forward gingerly into the midst of the electrical apparatus, and in less time than it takes to write it Lamar was hustled out to the doorway, each arm pinioned back of him.

As we stood, half dazed by the suddenness of the turn of events, Kennedy hastily explained:

"Tesla's theory is that under certain conditions the atmosphere, which is normally a high insulator; assumes conducting properties and so becomes capable of conveying any amount of electrical energy. I myself have seen electrical oscillations such as these in this room of such intensity that while they could be circulated with impunity through one's arms and chest they would melt wires farther along in the circuit. Yet the person through whom such a current is passing feels no inconvenience. I have seen a loop of heavy copper wire energised by such oscillations and a mass of metal within the loop heated to the fusing point, and yet into the space in which this destructive aerial turmoil was going on I have repeatedly thrust my hand and even my head, without feeling anything or experiencing any injurious after-effect. In this form all the energy of all the dynamos of Niagara could pass through one's body and yet produce no injury. But, diabolically directed, this vast energy has been used by this man to melt the wires in the little dynamo that runs Norton's gyroscope. That is all. Now to the aviation field. I have something more to show you."

We hurried as fast as we could up the street and straight out on the field, across toward the Norton hangar, the crowd gaping in wonderment. Kennedy waved frantically for Norton to come down, and Norton, who was only a few hundred feet in the air, seemed to see and understand.

As we stood waiting before the hangar Kennedy could no longer restrain his impatience.

"I suspected some wireless-power trick when I found that the field wireless telegraph failed to work every time Norton's aeroplane was in the air," he said, approaching close to Lamar. "I just happened to catch sight of that peculiar wireless mast of yours. A little flash of light first attracted my attention to it. I thought it was an electric spark, but you are too clever for that, Lamar. Still, you forgot a much simpler thing. It was the glint of the sun on the lens of your telescope as you were watching Norton that betrayed you."

Lamar said nothing.

"I'm glad to say you had no confederate in the hangar here," continued Craig. "At first I suspected it. Anyhow, you succeeded pretty well single handed, two lives lost and two machines wrecked. Norton flew all right yesterday when he left his gyroscope and dynamo behind, but when he took them along you were able to fuse the wires in the dynamo-- you pretty nearly succeeded in adding his name to those of Browne and Herrick."

The whir of Norton's machine told us he was approaching. We scattered to give him space enough to choose the spot where he would alight. As the men caught his machine to steady it, he jumped lightly to the ground.

"Where's Kennedy?" he asked, and then, without waiting for a reply, he exclaimed: "Queerest thing I ever saw up there. The dynamo wasn't protected by the sheet-lead shield in this flight as in the first to-day. I hadn't risen a hundred feet before I happened to hear the darndest sputtering in the dynamo. Look, boys, the insulation is completely burned off the wires, and the wires are nearly all fused together."

"So it was in the other two wrecked machines," added Kennedy, coming coolly forward. "If you hadn't had everything protected by those shields I gave you in your first flight to-day you would have simply repeated your fall of yesterday--perhaps fatally. This fellow has been directing the full strength of his wireless high-tension electricity straight at you all the time."

"What fellow?" demanded Norton.

The two Pinkertons shoved Lamar forward. Norton gave a contemptuous look at him. "Delanne," he said, "I knew you were a crook when you tried to infringe on my patent, but I didn't think you were coward enough to resort to--to murder."

Lamar, or rather Delanne, shrank back as if even the protection of his captors was safety compared to the threatening advance of Norton toward him.

"Pouff!" exclaimed Norton, turning suddenly on his heel. "What a fool I am! The law will take care of such scoundrels as you. What's the grand stand cheering for now?" he asked, looking across the field in an effort to regain his self-control.

A boy from one of the hangars down the line spoke up from the back of the crowd in a shrill, piping voice. "You have been awarded the Brooks Prize, sir," he said.